# ON MARDI GRAS DAY

## Fatima Shaik

### paintings by Floyd Cooper

## Dial Books for Young Readers

### New York

To my father, Mohamed J. Shaik, Ph.D., who
always stood tall and carried me on his shoulders
F.S.

For Tiffany
F.C.

Published by Dial Books for Young Readers
A division of Penguin Putnam Inc.
345 Hudson Street
New York, New York 10014

Text copyright © 1999 by Fatima Shaik
Paintings copyright © 1999 by Floyd Cooper
All rights reserved
Designed by Debora Smith
Printed in Hong Kong on acid-free paper
First Edition
10 9 8 7 6 5 4 3 2 1

Library of Congress Cataloging in Publication Data
Shaik, Fatima, date.
On Mardi Gras day/by Fatima Shaik; paintings by Floyd Cooper.
p. cm.
Summary: Two children participating in the traditional Mardi Gras
celebration see such sights as the Zulu and Rex parades, enjoying the songs,
bright costumes, and gigantic floats.
ISBN 0-8037-1442-4
[1. Mardi Gras—Fiction. 2. New Orleans (La.)—Fiction.]
I. Cooper, Floyd, ill. II. Title.
PZ7.S52785Oj 1999
[E]—dc21 97-10588 CIP AC

The pictures for this book were painted in oil on board.

Special thanks to Professor Maurice M. Martinez of the Department
of Specialty Studies, University of North Carolina at Wilmington,
for his critical review of the text, and to Allison "Tootie" Montana,
Big Chief of the Yellow Pocahontas, for allowing the portrayal
of one of his authentic costumes in this book.

In the pink dawn we rise and dress in costumes for this day of street parties.

Some children will make believe they are cowboys, cats, firefighters, or clowns. Brother and I are divers from the deep blue sea.

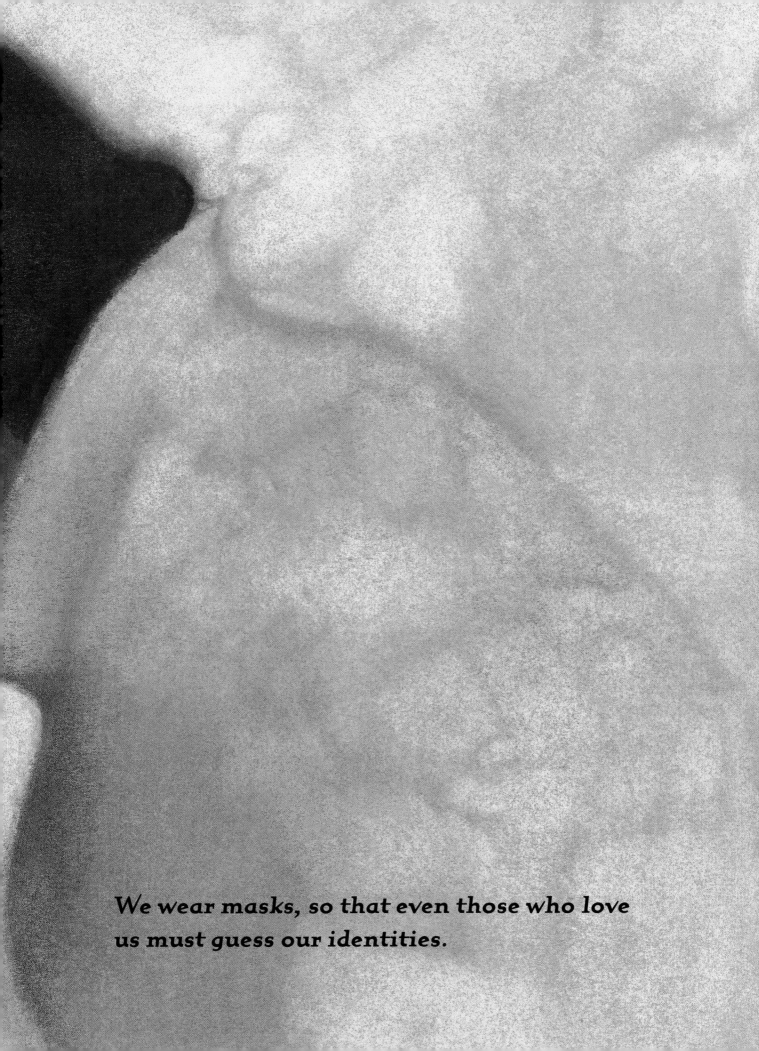

We wear masks, so that even those who love us must guess our identities.

"I know you, Mardi Gras," friends call when they catch us leaving our front step.

Mardi Gras Indians live in our neighborhood. Brother and I go to nearby streets to watch them start the day.

We cheer as each Indian comes out of the door blinds of his small house like a spring flower opening.

They wear costumes of bright colors with plumes, feathers, beads, and gemstones that shine like a million suns.

The Indians sew their beautiful suits by hand, and every year they make new ones.

We watch the Indians gather into a ring and chant, "Tu-way-pa-ka-way."

Their songs have been sung for a hundred years, taught by neighbor to neighbor and father to son.

We join their widening circle and sing in the chorus. It is our way of saying, "Yes! We are part of your memories and fun."

The gathering grows and gets louder. The beating of tambourines follows us as we go back to our house.

Papa drives us in the truck to Nanan's.
A parade named Zulu will pass in front
of her high porch.

We wait for a long time on Nanan's balcony.

"Here comes Zulu now!" Brother shouts.
This parade makes fun of some old Southern
traditions that once kept white and black
people apart.

The parade that follows is named Rex.

We walk to Canal Street to see the gigantic
floats. They glide past us like tinsel ships.

On them are people in pastel jumpsuits, giant headpieces, and satin masks.

They pitch us beads and fake coins called doubloons. We holler, "Mister! Throw me something!" to every moving thing.

By noon we are inside the house to
eat gumbo, potato salad, ham and peas,
hot dogs and chili, fried chicken, and
chocolate cake.

We make jokes and bless the cook.

Then everybody has an afternoon sleep.

We wake up one by one to hear kids under
the window throwing beads to each other
and blowing plastic horns.

We play marching band in the backyard.
Like the St. Augustine Marching 100, we
can turn, lift one leg, and arch our backs—
and still keep the right musical beat.

When night falls, Papa takes us walking to Canal Street to catch the final parade.

We hear whistles and sirens before we see anything, even from his shoulders, in the pitch-safe dark.

A river of lights, noise, and music flows
quickly to us, then away down the street.

The last lamp dancers carry the holiday out.

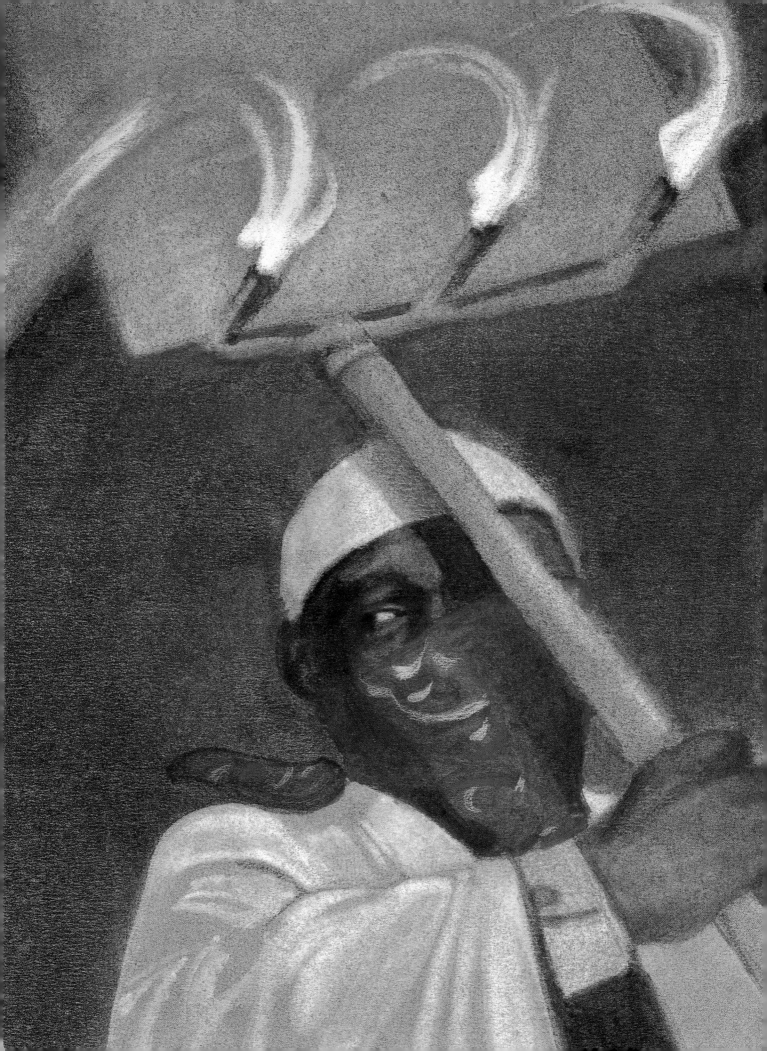

# Author's Note

Mardi Gras in New Orleans is a street festival for the whole city. Most everyone goes to the parades, and many people wear costumes. *Mardi Gras* is French for "Fat Tuesday." It is the last day of eating and drinking in excess before the Christian fasting season of Lent. The Mardi Gras season of good times and parties begins every "Kings' Day" (also called Twelfth Night), on January 6.

The Mardi Gras Indians are groups of friends who make up "tribes" through their shared songs and traditions. Every Mardi Gras they dress in costumes of colorful feathers and beads to walk through the city's black communities, stopping often to dance to the beat of tambourines and to sing with their neighbors. The headdresses (called crowns), fringed "suits," and beaded aprons worn by the Mardi Gras Indians most closely resemble Native American articles of dress. The costumes' colors and designs may also show traces of African culture—but the Mardi Gras Indians are unique to New Orleans.

An Indian creates an original suit every year. He chooses a new combination of feathers and plumes in a flamboyant hue to attach to his costume, and he sketches out designs for the glittering beads and gemstones he will sew on by hand. The long hours spent in pattern making and expert sewing to put the costume together are a source of honor and pride for every tribe member. The Indians show how cultures survive; they have been around for over a hundred years. When laws existed forbidding blacks to meet in groups or in public, some New Orleanians—many of whom were of African or Native American descent—used Mardi Gras Day as an opportunity to freely celebrate their traditions. In costume, people came together and communicated with each other in African and Native American dialects and songs. They passed on information to each other through call-and-response singing, and to the beat of drums heavily influenced by African rhythms. Over time these people organized themselves into tribes.

Today important members of a tribe are the "Big Chief" and the "Flagboy," who carries the tribe's colors and announces the Chief's arrival. The "Spyboy" scouts ahead of their march to make sure the streets are clear. Children who live near the Indians might be the first to watch their special processions on Mardi Gras Day. All this happens early, even before the morning parades begin.

The first procession of floats to reach New Orleans' main street for everyone's enjoyment is Zulu. It shows the city's black pride, but in a humorous way. Club members who ride the floats dress in grass skirts and wear blackface. It is their way of making fun of the laws that did not allow blacks to join carnival clubs many years ago. The next parade that everyone sees is Rex. It takes itself very seriously as the parade of the city's "aristocrats."

More festivities are shared by tourists and the people of New Orleans all day and into the evening. And exactly at midnight, people unmask and go home because Mardi Gras ends.